_____ 36 ft

_____ 30 ft

_____ 24 ft

_____ 18 ft

_____ 12 ft

_____ 6 ft

Tyrannosaurus rex   **Velociraptor**

Dinosaurs

Bloz • Art
Arnaud Plumeri • Story
Maëla Cosson • Color

New York

Dinosaurs Graphic Novels Available from PAPERCUTZ™

Coming Soon! **Coming Soon!**

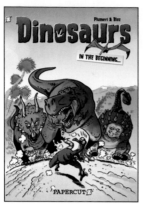 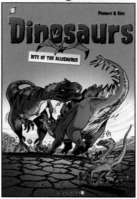 

Graphic Novel #1
"In the Beginning…"

Graphic Novel #2
"Bite of the Allosaurus"

Graphic Novel #3
"Jurassic Smarts"

Dinosaurs

Dinosaures [Dinosaurs] by Arnaud Plumeri & Bloz
© 2010 BAMBOO ÉDITION.
www.bamboo.fr
All other editorial material © 2013 by Papercutz.

DINOSAURS #1
"In the Beginning…"

Arnaud Plumeri – Writer
Bloz – Artist
Maëla Cosson – Colorist
Nanette McGuinness – Translation
Janice Chiang – Letterer
Dawn K. Guzzo – Production
Beth Scorzato – Production Coordinator
Michael Petranek – Editor
Jim Salicrup
Editor-in-Chief

ISBN: 978-1-59707-490-2

Printed in China
December 2013 by WKT Co. LTD
3/F Phase I Leader Industrial Centre
188 Texaco Road, Tseun Wan, N.T., Hong Kong

Papercutz books may be purchased for business or promotional use.
For information on bulk purchases please contact Macmillan Corporate and
Premium Sales Department at (800) 221-7945 x5442.

Distributed by Macmillan
First Papercutz Printing

DINOSAURS graphic novels are available for $10.99 only in hardcover. Available from booksellers everywhere. You can also order online from papercutz.com Or call 1-800-886-1223, Monday through Friday, 9 – 5 EST. MC, Visa, and AmEx accepted. To order by mail, please add $4.00 for postage and handling for first book ordered, $1.00 for each additional book and make check payable to NBM Publishing. Send to: Papercutz, 160 Broadway, Suite 700, East Wing, New York, NY 10038.

DINOSAURS graphic novels are also available digitally wherever e-books are sold.

Papercutz.com

RECORDS

YOU WANT TO LEARN ABOUT DINOSAUR RECORDS? ASK INDINO JONES!

THAT'S ME, HEE, HEE!

FASTEST DINOSAUR? GALLIMIMUS, WITH SPRINTS OF UP TO 40 MPH!

PTOUEK! PTOUEK!

YUCK!

UGH! THE PROBLEM IS THAT I SWALLOW LOTS OF MOSQUITOES!

LONGEST DINOSAUR? ARGENTINOSAURUS, NO DOUBT-- 130 FEET LONG!

AND AS FOR CARNIVORES, GIGANOTOSAURUS WAS ONE OF THE MOST MASSIVE (46 FEET, 17,636 LBS).

YUM! THERE'S AT LEAST A YEAR OF GRUB OVER THERE!

SMALLEST DINOSAUR? MICRORAPTOR-- 16 INCHES LONG!

HEY! THAT'S NO REASON TO STICK ME IN A TINY LITTLE PANEL!

SMARTEST DINOSAUR? TROODON WAS AS SMART AS A CAT!

UEE! HEE!

THAT'S WHY I BURY MY DROPPINGS!

DUMBEST DINOSAUR? STEGOSAURUS, WITH A BRAIN THE SIZE OF A WALNUT!

DON'T GO THAT WAY, YOU BIG DOPE! THE VOLCANO'S ERUPTING!

DUH...?

WHICH HAD THE BIGGEST HEAD? TOROSAURUS*, WITH A SKULL THAT WAS 10 FEET LONG AND WEIGHED 4,000 LBS.!

TALK ABOUT A STIFF NECK...

OH, YEAH! BECAUSE, IN MY OPINION, SOMEONE WHO REALLY HAS A BIG HEAD...

IS A GUY WHO REFUSES TO TAKE OUT THE TRASH OR WALK THE DOG!

IF IT'S A QUESTION OF LAZINESS, YOU BREAK ALL THE RECORDS!

CALM DOWN, DEAREST, I'M GOING!

*EXPERTS HAVE FOUND THAT TOROSAURUS MIGHT HAVE ACTUALLY BEEN AN ADULT TRICERATOPS.

THE FIRST DINOSAURS

WELCOME TO THE *TRIASSIC*, 230 MILLION YEARS AGO...

HEY, GUYS! COME SEE WHAT I FOUND!

SOME OLD REPTILES BUMP INTO SOMETHING THAT WILL CHANGE THEIR LIVES...

I MUST BE SEEING THINGS.

WHAT'S THIS IRRITATING THINGAMAJIG?

HUH?

...ONE OF THE FIRST DINOSAURS: *EORAPTOR.*

HOW ABOUT A LITTLE RESPECT, GUYS!

I DON'T SEE ANYTHING SPECIAL ABOUT THIS DINO-THINGY...

IS THAT A JOKE, BUDDY?!

FIRST OF ALL, I WALK ON TWO LEGS...

...WHICH NOT EVERYONE GETS TO DO...

BZZZZ

AND WHICH LETS ME BE SUPER SWIFT WHEN HUNTING!

CLAP

GULP

PLUS I'VE GOT POTENTIAL!

IN A FEW YEARS, I'VE GOT A HUNCH I'M GOING TO BECOME EXTRA HUGE!

GROW RR

T. Rex

NO WAY!

GO ON, GET OUTTA HERE!

JUST A FAD, THESE DINOSAURS!

BURP

THAT'S NEVER GOING TO HAPPEN!

HOPE-LESS!

WHAT AN IDIOT!

YOU'RE NOT GOING TO BE SO BIG IN A FEW MILLION YEARS!

SADLY FOR THEM, THESE OLD REPTILES WILL SOON GIVE WAY TO THE AMBITIOUS DINOSAURS.

PLUMERI / BLOZ

TYRANNOSAURUS REX

LET'S TAKE A LOOK AT THIS SULLEN LITTLE DINOSAUR...

HEY, GUYS, CHECK OUT WHO'S TURNED UP! IT'S THE LITTLE RUNT!

HI, LITTLE RUNT! YOU'RE UGLY, YOU KNOW THAT?

...IT DOESN'T LOOK LIKE HE HAS AN EASY LIFE...

SO, UGLY DUCKLING, YOU'RE WALKING AROUND LIKE A GROWNUP?

YOU DO KNOW YOU COULD GET YOURSELF INTO SOME TROUBLE?

≶GRUMMBLLLE≶

GET OUT OF MY TERRITORY, YOU UGLY, LITTLE RUNT!

YUM! A JUICY LITTLE FLEDGLING!

WAAAH!

FLAP FLAP FLAP

SUCH TRAGIC SCENES. BUT SOON THE TABLES WILL TURN!

AT ADOLESCENCE, OUR LITTLE DINOSAUR WILL LOSE HIS FEATHERS....

?

AND WILL GROW AND GROW INTO A TERRIFYING TYRANNOSAURUS REX!

ROAR

A DIFFICULT CHILDHOOD... COULD THAT BE THE REASON FOR T. REX'S NASTY TEMPER? IT'S A MYSTERY!

WHY'S HE SO MEAN?

ROOO OAR

TYRANNOSAURUS REX

MEANING: TYRANT LIZARD KING
PERIOD: LATE CRETACEOUS (68-65 MILLION YEARS AGO)
ORDER/ FAMILY: SAURISCHIA / TYRANNOSAURIDAE
SIZE: 35-50 FEET LONG
WEIGHT: 11,000 POUNDS
DIET: CARNIVORE
FOUND: NORTH AMERICA

T. PLUMERI & BUOZ-REX

WHAT'S A DINOSAUR?

DINOSAUR IS A TERM INVENTED BY *SIR RICHARD OWEN*. IT MEANS "FEARFULLY GREAT LIZARD," IN GREEK.

"FEARFULLY GREAT LIZARD?" HA! HE MUST HAVE NEVER MET YOU, COMPSO!

WE'VE IDENTIFIED OVER 1000 DINOSAUR SPECIES, AND PALEONTOLOGISTS DISCOVER ABOUT A DOZEN MORE EVERY YEAR.

OBSERVE, "LITTLE GUY!" HERE'S MY LATEST DISCOVERY...

...A FRAGMENT OF THE SKULL OF A FEMALE FLEABAGASUS!

UH, BOSS... I THINK THAT'S JUST A DRIED COW PATTY...

THESE CREATURES RULED THE EARTH FOR A LONG PERIOD: FROM BETWEEN 230-65 MILLION YEARS AGO. THUS, TYRANNOSAURUS DID NOT LIVE IN THE SAME TIME PERIOD AS COMPSOGNATHUS...

‹PHEW!› THAT'S A RELIEF!

UNFORTUNATELY FOR THEM, COMPSOGNATHUS COULD ENCOUNTER ANOTHER MONSTER: ALLOSAURUS...

ALLOSAURUS?! THIS IS WORSE!

MOMMY!

UNLIKE TODAY'S REPTILES, DINOSAURS DID NOT CRAWL: THEY WALKED UPRIGHT ON 2 OR 4 LEGS.

ARE YOU GOING TO CRAWL BEFORE YOUR MASTER, LITTLE WORM?

ON MY MOTHER'S LIFE, I CAN'T, SIR! SCIENCE SAYS SO!

AS FOR DIET, SOME DINOSAURS WERE *HERBIVORES* (PLANT EATERS) AND OTHERS WERE *CARNIVORES* (MEAT EATERS).

I'M NOT PICKY! I LIKE *ALL* DINOSAURS!

BUT I'M TELLING YOU I TASTE AWFUL!

HELP!

WITH SPINES, HORNS, AND ARMOR, DINOSAURS COULD HAVE GREATLY DIFFERING AND SURPRISING APPEARANCES...

THAT'S REALLY ORIGINAL!

A REAL EGGHEAD!

HELP ME CRACK THIS SHELL INSTEAD OF CRACKING UP!

HO HO HO

HEH HEH HEH

AS FAR AS THE COLOR OF DINOSAURS GOES, WE CAN ONLY GUESS.

TOO GAUDY TO HIDE!

THIS COLOR'S GREAT FOR FLIRTING.

WHEN I TURN RED, YOU'D BETTER NOT COME LOOKING FOR ME!

YIKES!

SCRAW

SCRAW

RECENTLY, WE'VE FIGURED OUT THAT CERTAIN SPECIES, SUCH AS VELOCIRAPTORS, HAD FEATHERS...

YIPPEE! I'M THE KING OF THE WORLD!

BUT THEY WERE MORE FOR STAYING WARM THAN FOR FLYING.

WAAA FLOP

DURING THIS PERIOD, THE SEAS WERE ALSO FILLED WITH FEARSOME CREATURES SUCH AS THE GIGANTIC *LIOPLEURODON* HERE...

THAT'S BECAUSE I HAVE 80 FEET OF BODY TO FEED, KIDS!

AND WITH *PTEROSAURS*, THE SKIES WEREN'T LEFT EMPTY, EITHER.

FLY ME TO THE MOON-- LET ME PLAY AMONG THE STARS!

I WANT TO FLY AWAY FROM YOUR SONGS!

NOTE, HOWEVER, THAT LIOPLEURODON AND PTEROSAURS WERE MARINE AND FLYING REPTILES, AND NOT DINOSAURS!

DINOSAUR OR NOT, WHAT DIFFERENCE DOES IT MAKE?! I'LL BE GOBBLED UP EITHER WAY!

IT'S HARD, HARD, ⸱AARGH⸱ BEING A DINOSAUR!

RAINERI 8 BLOZ

TROODON

LET'S GET TO KNOW THE *TROODON*...

OOH, LA, LA! WHAT DO I SEE?

A DINOSAUR THAT NOTICES EVERYTHING THAT ISN'T QUITE RIGHT...

WHATEVER ARE YOU DOING, TRICERATOPS!

BUT HIS MAIN CHARACTERISTIC IS INTELLIGENCE...

YOU'RE GOING TO BREAK YOUR HORNS AND THEY'RE YOUR ONLY WAY TO DEFEND YOURSELVES!

VERY INTELLIGENT...

AND YOU, THERE-- DO YOU WANT TO GET FOOD POISONING? WHY ARE YOU EATING ROTTEN FERNS?

THERE ARE FRESH PLANTS RIGHT OVER THERE!

HMMM?

TAP TAP

CHROMPP GUKROMP GUKROMP

AND HE LIKES TO MAKE THAT KNOWN...

IT'S NOT VERY SMART TO EAT HIM NOW, REX!

?

?

WAIT ANOTHER MONTH BEFORE NABBING HIM!

THAT WAY, HE'LL HAVE FATTENED UP NICELY AND YOU'LL HAVE TO CHASE HIM MUCH LESS!

BUT IN A WORLD OF BRUTES, IS THERE ROOM FOR BRAINS?

LEAVE US ALONE, NERD!

I'LL GET SNACKED ON WHEN I WANT!

YOU KNOW WHAT MY HORNS ARE TELLING YOU?

TROODON

MEANING: WOUNDING TOOTH
PERIOD: LATE CRETACEOUS (75-65 MILLION YEARS AGO)
ORDER/ FAMILY: SAURISCHIA/ TROODONTIDAE
SIZE: 6.5 FEET LONG
WEIGHT: 110 LBS.
DIET: CARNIVORE
FOUND: NORTH AMERICA

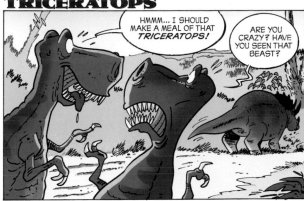

HMMM... I SHOULD MAKE A MEAL OF THAT *TRICERATOPS!*

ARE YOU CRAZY? HAVE YOU SEEN THAT BEAST?

WITH ITS POWERFUL PHYSIQUE, IT CAN DESTROY EVERYTHING IN ITS PATH.

CRUNCH CRUNCH YUM...

NOT TO MENTION ITS SKULL, WHICH IS REINFORCED WITH A BONY COLLAR...

CRUNCH CRUNCH

AND WORST OF ALL: THREE HORNS THAT ARE SHARP AS KNIVES!

:SNIFF!:

?

I KNOW ALL THAT! BUT IT'S SO GOOD, AND SUPER PRACTICAL FOR EATING!

SUPER PRACTICAL?

EEEK!

ROAR

OWIE! *ROAR* YUM ARGH! *GROW* OUCH! CRUMP

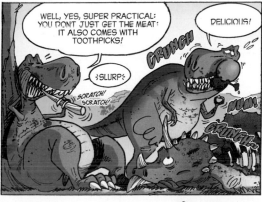

WELL, YES, SUPER PRACTICAL: YOU DON'T JUST GET THE MEAT: IT ALSO COMES WITH TOOTHPICKS!

DELICIOUS!

:SLURP:

SCRATCH! SCRATCH!

CRUNCH

YUM

CRUNCH

TRICERATOPS

MEANING: THREE-HORNED FACE
PERIOD: LATE CRETACEOUS (68-65 MILLION YEARS AGO)
ORDER/ FAMILY: ORNITHISCHIA/ CERATOPSIDAE
SIZE: 30 FEET LONG
WEIGHT: 20,000 LBS.
DIET: HERBIVORE
FOUND: NORTH AMERICA

FAMOUS DINOSAURS OF THE JURASSIC

THE FIRST DINOSAUR FROM THE JURASSIC TO BECOME FAMOUS WAS ALSO THE FIRST TO BE NAMED, IN 1824: *MEGALOSAURUS*.

ITS COUSIN, *ALLOSAURUS*, WAS A "MINIATURE" TYRANNOSAURUS REX-- BUT STILL 35 FEET LONG WITH 70 TEETH!

CAMPTOSAURUS WAS LIKE A BIG COW THAT COULD DIGEST EVERY PLANT WITHIN REACH.

AS FOR *STEGOSAURUS*, IT'S WELL KNOWN FOR ITS DORSAL PLATES AND SPIKED TAIL.

A REAL TITAN, *BRACHIOSAURUS* TOWERED OVER ITS ERA, MEASURING 80 FEET LONG AND WEIGHING 110,000 POUNDS!

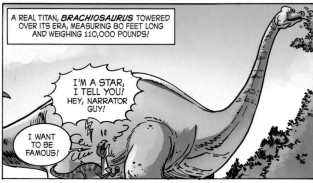

HERE'S THE SKELETON OF A YOUNG COMPSOGNATHUS. ITS BONES WERE CRUSHED FOR SOME UNKNOWN REASON...

COMPSOGNATHUS

THE PROUD DINOSAUR YOU'RE LOOKING AT IS A *COMPSOGNATHUS*.

YUP, AND THAT MEANS, "ELEGANT JAW," TOO.

DON'T BE MISLED BY ITS DELICATE APPEARANCE. YOU'RE DEALING WITH A PEERLESS HUNTER!

CHECK OUT THE TECHNIQUE, KIDS.

THANKS TO ITS PROTRUDING EYES, IT CAN DETECT ITS PREY FROM A DISTANCE.

YUM! A LOVELY DRAGONFLY!

AND THAT'S WHEN IT USES ITS REMARKABLE AGILITY AND SPRINGS INTO ACTION...

HOP HOP HOP HOP

COMPSOGNATHUS IS MADE FOR SPEED-- ESTIMATED AT OVER 35 MILES/HOUR.

SO IT'S IMPOSSIBLE TO ESCAPE HIM WHEN HE'S GOT YOU IN HIS LINE OF SIGHT!

BANZAI!

BUT THE MOST IMPORTANT DETAIL: COMPSOGNATHUS ISN'T BIGGER THAN A CHICKEN...

NOT TO MENTION THE GIANT INSECTS OF THE JURASSIC!

YUM! A COMPSOGNATHUS!

I'M SO ASHAMED.

COMPSOGNATHUS

MEANING: ELEGANT JAW
PERIOD: LATE JURASSIC (156-140 MILLION YEARS AGO)
ORDER/ FAMILY: SAURISCHIA/ COMPSOGNATHIDAE
SIZE: 3 FEET LONG
WEIGHT: 6 1/2 LBS.
DIET: CARNIVORE
FOUND: GERMANY, FRANCE

ERAS

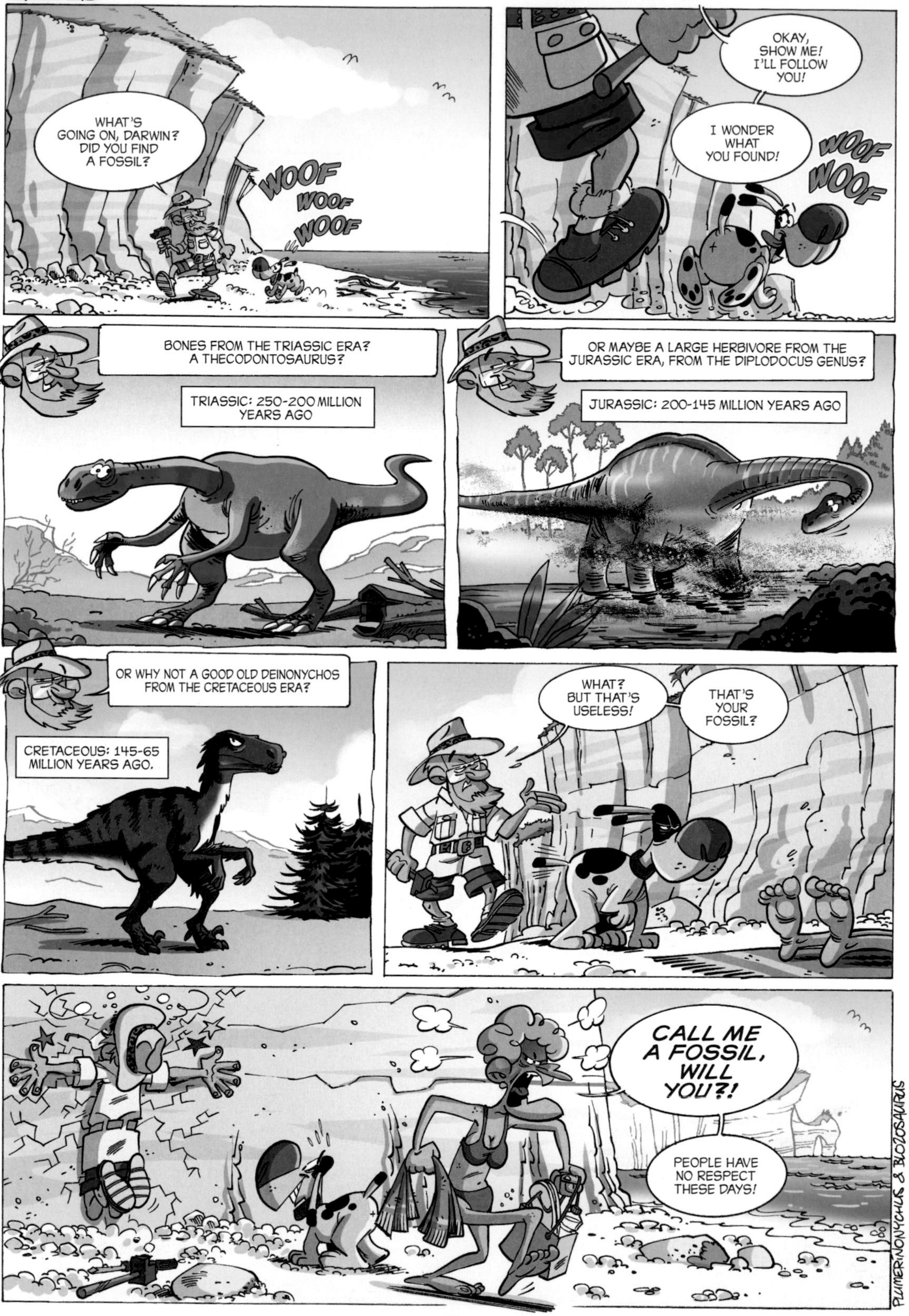

WHAT'S GOING ON, DARWIN? DID YOU FIND A FOSSIL?
WOOF
WOOF
WOOF
OKAY, SHOW ME! I'LL FOLLOW YOU!
I WONDER WHAT YOU FOUND!
WOOF
WOOF
BONES FROM THE TRIASSIC ERA? A THECODONTOSAURUS?
TRIASSIC: 250-200 MILLION YEARS AGO
OR MAYBE A LARGE HERBIVORE FROM THE JURASSIC ERA, FROM THE DIPLODOCUS GENUS?
JURASSIC: 200-145 MILLION YEARS AGO
OR WHY NOT A GOOD OLD DEINONYCHOS FROM THE CRETACEOUS ERA?
CRETACEOUS: 145-65 MILLION YEARS AGO.
WHAT? BUT THAT'S USELESS!
THAT'S YOUR FOSSIL?
CALL ME A FOSSIL, WILL YOU?!
PEOPLE HAVE NO RESPECT THESE DAYS!
PLUMERINONYCHUS & BLOZOSAURUS

STEGOSAURUS

150 MILLION YEARS AGO, THE WORLD WAS FILLED WITH STEGOSAURUSES...

HI!

HI!

HEY!

ONE OF THE STRANGEST HERBIVORES OF THE JURASSIC.

HEY, CAMPTOSAURS, COME OVER AND GRAZE ON THE FERNS! THEY'RE SUPER TENDER!

ON MY WAY!

MUNCH CRUNCH

TO FRIGHTEN ITS ENEMIES, ITS IMPOSING DORSAL PLATES FILLED UP WITH BLOOD AND TOOK ON A BRIGHT RED SHADE.

JUST WHO DO YOU THINK YOU ARE? GET AWAY FROM HERE!

WH-- WHAT?

STEGOSAURUS LIKED TO FEED ON TENDER PLANTS.

HEY, CAMPTO! COME OVER AND GRAZE ON THESE FERNS! THEY'RE SUPER TENDER!

WHAT? WELL... OKAY!

YUM CRUNCH

ITS TAIL WAS EQUIPPED WITH FRIGHTENING SPIKES, VERY USEFUL IN CASE OF DANGER.

DON'T TOUCH MY FERNS! THEY'RE MINE!

WHUMP!

BUT--

ANOTHER CHARACTERISTIC OF STEGOSAURUS...

HEY, CAMPTO! COME OVER AND GRAZE ON THESE FERNS! THEY'RE SUPER TENDER!

HE'S EITHER CRAZY, STUPID, OR BOTH!

THE STEGOSAURUS'S BRAIN WAS NO BIGGER THAN A WALNUT-- WHICH LEADS US TO DOUBT IT HAD ANY REAL INTELLIGENCE...

DON'T TOUCH MY FERNS, STRANGER!

ANY DUMBER, YOU'D BE DEAD!

Stegosaurus

MEANING: ROOF LIZARD
PERIOD: LATE JURASSIC (156-140 MILLION YEARS AGO)
ORDER/ FAMILY: ORNITHISCHIAN/ STEGOSAURIDAE
SIZE: 30 FEET LONG
WEIGHT: 11,000 POUNDS
DIET: HERBIVORE
FOUND: NORTH AMERICA

PLUMERI - BLOZ

HOW ARE FOSSILS FORMED?

SOMEWHERE IN THE UNITED STATES, 65 MILLION YEARS AGO...

REX MAKES A SURPRISE ATTACK...!

EEEK!

SNAP!

THIS POOR PARASAUROLOPHUS DOESN'T SUSPECT HE'S ABOUT TO BECOME A PRICELESS FOSSIL.

ON SECOND THOUGHT-- I'M NOT THAT HUNGRY!

GAAK...! I'M DYING!

THE DINOSAUR'S BODY QUICKLY SINKS INTO THE LAKE AND IS COVERED WITH SAND...

THE DINOSAUR DECOMPOSES. THE SAND TURNS INTO ROCK AND SOLIDIFIES THE DINOSAUR'S BONES INTO STONE. THIS IS "FOSSILIZATION."

IN THE SAME PLACE, IN OUR TIME, THE FOSSIL ENDS UP RISING TO THE SURFACE OF THE EARTH.

I THINK I'VE GOT ONE, DARWIN!

I'M SO GOOD!

SCRATCH

EUREKA! COME AND SEE, MY DOGGIE DOG!

AN ENORMOUS BONE! WHAT A FIND!

SNAP

AH... HMMM... ...GOOD

UH. NEVER MIND.

ARF! ARF!

PALMERI & BLOZ

DEINONYCHUS

MEANING: TERRIBLE CLAW
PERIOD: EARLY CRETACEOUS (120-98 MILLION YEARS AGO)
ORDER/ FAMILY: SAURISCHIA/ DROMAEOSAURIDAE
SIZE: 10 FEET LONG
WEIGHT: 175 LBS.
DIET: CARNIVORE
FOUND: NORTH AMERICA

BRACHIOSAURUS

FROM THE TIME THEY'RE BORN AND THROUGHOUT THEIR LIVES, BRACHIOSAURS HAVE A SINGLE OBSESSION...

WE'RE HUNGRY...

EATING!

MOMMY!

INDEED, THE BIGGER THEY GET, THE MORE EASILY THEY CAN KEEP THEIR PREDATORS AWAY!

MOVE OUT OF THE WAY. I NEED TO EAT!

WELL, ME, TOO!

ONCE THEY GROW BIG ENOUGH, THE BRACHIOSAURS GET BACK TOGETHER AND FORM A HERD, IN SEARCH OF FOOD.

I'M HUNGRY!

OH, YOU, TOO?

WHEN ARE WE GOING TO EAT?

IS IT STILL FAR TO OUR GRUB?

BE PATIENT, I KNOW OF A GREAT SPOT!

THE GREAT SPOT: A LUSH JURASSIC FOREST...

WELCOME TO MY FOREST, BRACHIOS!

FOR AN APPETIZER, I RECOMMEND THE HORSETAILS...

VERY CRUNCHY...

FOR THE MAIN COURSE, FERNS AL DENTE, FOLLOWED BY--

THANKS FOR THE INVITATION, CAMPTO!

I'M STILL HUNGRY!

MY FOREST! MY BEAUTIFUL FOREST!

CRUNCH

WHEREVER THE BRACHIOSAURUS PASS, THE TREES PASS AWAY!

Brachiosaurus

MEANING: ARM LIZARD
PERIOD: LATE JURASSIC (160-145 MILLION YEARS AGO)
ORDER/ FAMILY: SAURISCHIA/ BRACHIOSAURIDAE
SIZE: 80 FEET LONG
WEIGHT: 110,000 LBS.
DIET: HERBIVORE
FOUND: AFRICA, AMERICA, EUROPE

PLUMERI- BK02

THE CONTINENTAL DRIFT

PANIC AMONG THE DINOSAURS! THE EARTH WAS SHAKING; THE CONTINENTS WERE MOVING...

...CAUSING NUMEROUS VOLCANIC ERUPTIONS.

I'VE HAD ENOUGH OF THESE CONTINENTS THAT WON'T STOP DRIFTING!

TRIASSIC: 250 MILLION YEARS AGO, THE EARTH ONLY HAD ONE IMMENSE CONTINENT, PANGEA.

JURASSIC: 150 MILLION YEARS AGO, THE SUPERCONTINENT BEGAN TO BREAK UP.

CRETACEOUS: 65 MILLION YEARS AGO, THE EARTH WAS DIVIDED INTO SEVERAL LARGE CONTINENTS.

SEPARATED ON THEIR RESPECTIVE CONTINENTS, SPECIES EVOLVED INTO VERY DIFFERENT SHAPES. SO IN THE JURASSIC, WE COULD FIND...

MAMENCHISAURUS AND GUANLONG IN CHINA.

ORNITHOLESTES AND STEGOSAURUS IN NORTH AMERICA.

GROWRR

AAAHH!

ALLOSAURUS AND COMPSOGNATHUS IN EUROPE.

SAVED! A LITTLE ISLAND!

BYE BYE, LOSER!

CONTINENTAL DRIFT IS SO HANDY!

HEH, HEH

PLUMERI - BLOZ

DUNG BEETLES

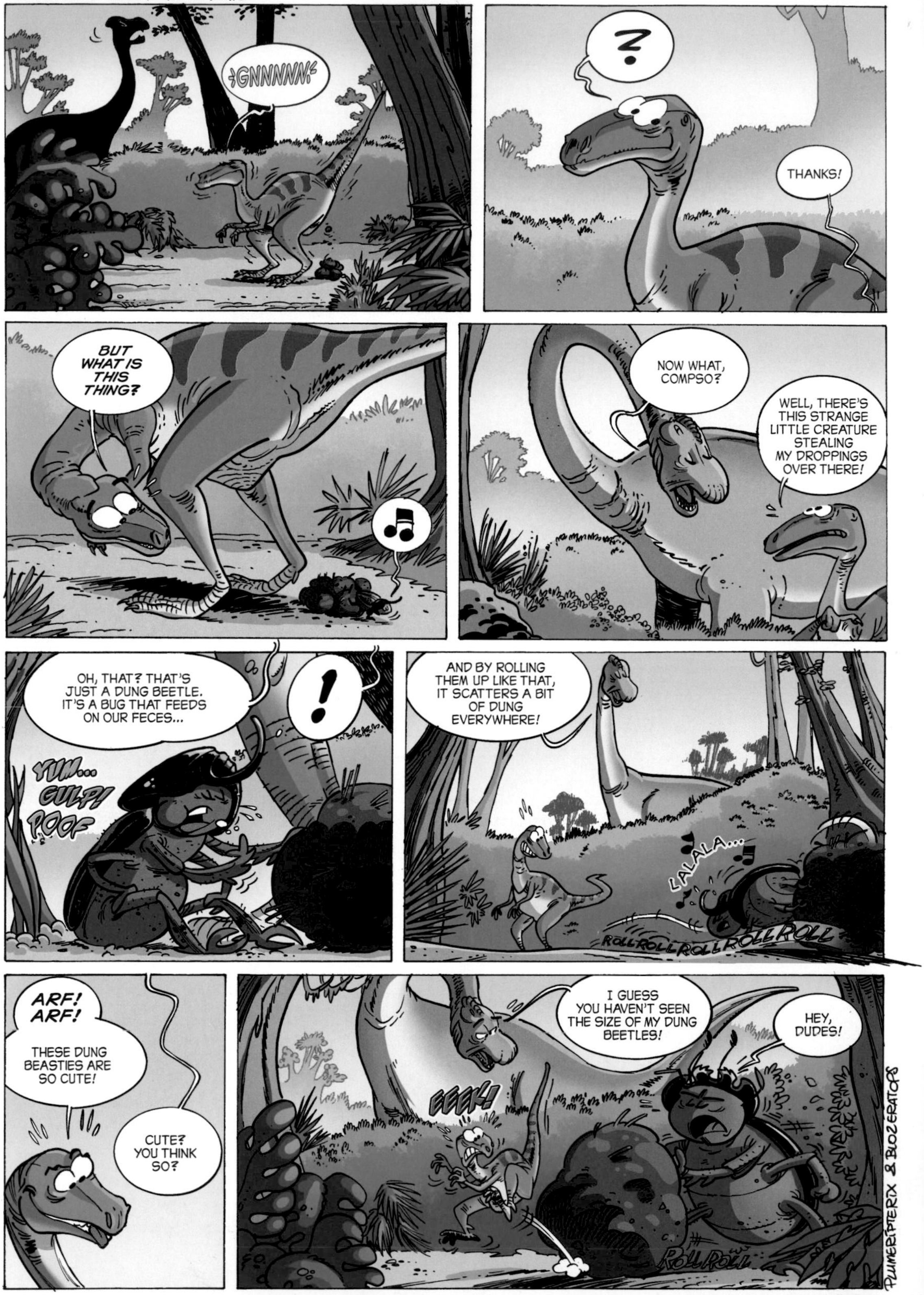
GNNNNN!
?
THANKS!
BUT WHAT IS THIS THING?
NOW WHAT, COMPSO?
WELL, THERE'S THIS STRANGE LITTLE CREATURE STEALING MY DROPPINGS OVER THERE!
OH, THAT? THAT'S JUST A DUNG BEETLE. IT'S A BUG THAT FEEDS ON OUR FECES...
!
YUM... GULP! POOF
AND BY ROLLING THEM UP LIKE THAT, IT SCATTERS A BIT OF DUNG EVERYWHERE!
LALALA...
ROLL ROLL ROLL ROLL ROLL
ARF! ARF!
THESE DUNG BEASTIES ARE SO CUTE!
CUTE? YOU THINK SO?
I GUESS YOU HAVEN'T SEEN THE SIZE OF MY DUNG BEETLES!
HEY, DUDES!
EEEK!
ROLL ROLL
PLUMERIPTERIX & BLOZERATOPS

SPINOSAURUS VS. TYRANNOSAURUS REX

ON OUR LEFT, THE FEARSOME TYRANNOSAURUS REX, AT 40 FEET LONG AND WEIGHING 10,000 LBS.!

CHECK OUT THE KING OF THE DINOS!

ON OUR RIGHT, THE ABOMINABLE SPINOSAURUS, AT 50 FEET LONG AND WEIGHING 15,000 LBS.!

NO ONE CAN STAND UP TO ME!

T. REX: 8 INCH-LONG DAGGER-LIKE TEETH AND AN UNMATCHED KNOWLEDGE OF FIGHTING!

IF YOU'RE LOOKING FOR A BRAWL, YOU FOUND ONE!

SPINOSAURUS: AN ENORMOUS CROCODILE MOUTH AND A TERRIFYING DORSAL CREST!

WE'RE GOING TO DO JUST THAT!

WHO WILL EMERGE THE VICTOR IN THIS CLASH OF THE TITANS?

WHERE'D HE GO? WHERE'D HE GO? I'M GOING TO GOBBLE HIM UP!

NO ONE, BECAUSE THESE TWO DINOSAURS CAN'T HAVE CROSSED EACH OTHER'S PATHS-- THEY NEVER EXISTED IN THE SAME PERIOD!

WHAT?

UM... HE SAID THE FIGHT WAS IMPOSSIBLE!

OH, REALLY?

TOO BAD FOR YOU-- I DIDN'T GET WORKED UP FOR NOTHING!

SPINOSAURUS

MEANING: SPINY REPTILE
PERIOD: LATE CRETACEOUS (108-94 MILLION YEARS AGO)
ORDER/ FAMILY: SAURISCHIA/ SPINOSAURIDAE
SIZE: 50 FEET LONG
WEIGHT: 15,000 LBS.
DIET: CARNIVORE AND PISCIVORE
FOUND: NORTHERN AFRICA

ONCE UPON A TIME, IN PORTUGAL...

BE GOOD, MY LITTLE EGGS! MAMA'S GOING TO GO GET SOMETHING TO DRINK!

SO WHERE ARE THOSE LITTLE EGGS?!

YUM!

GULP

WOAH!

I'M GOING TO HAVE MYSELF A GREAT MEAL!

CRRR

PLOCK...

TICK

CRACK

BLACK

CRACK...

CRRRR...

RRRWEEER

RWEER

RWEER

RWEER

RWEER

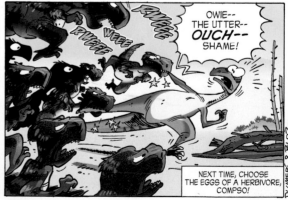

RWEER

WEEE

RWEER

OWIE-- THE UTTER-- OUCH-- SHAME!

NEXT TIME, CHOOSE THE EGGS OF A HERBIVORE, COMPSO!

THERIZINOSAURUS

THERIZINOSAURUS

MEANING: SCYTHE LIZARD
PERIOD: LATE CRETACEOUS (70-65 MILLION YEARS AGO)
ORDER/ FAMILY: SAURISCHIA/ THERIZINOSAURIDAE
SIZE: 30 FEET LONG
WEIGHT: 13,000 LBS.
DIET: HERBIVORE
FOUND: CHINA, MONGOLIA

PLUMERI & BIOZ

IGUANODON

SCENE FROM THE CRETACEOUS. A *NEOVENATOR* IS PURSUING A PEACEFUL *IGUANODON*...

WHY ME?

I'VE GOT SOMETHING FOR YOU! IN FACT, I'VE GOT 70 SOMETHINGS IN MY MOUTH!

THE IGUANODON, A DEFENSELESS HERBIVORE?

UNCLE! LET'S STOP!

?

SKREEE

NOT QUITE, THANKS TO ITS EXTRA-POINTY THUMBS!

OW!

HEY THERE! HERE'S A HELPING HAND!

SPROTCH

THE IGUANODON WAS A VERY COMMON DINOSAUR THAT LIKED TO GRAZE IN HERDS.

HOW'RE THE HORSE-TAILS?

MAGNIFIQUE!

GNAMPH

GNOMPH GHO

WE'VE KNOWN ABOUT IT SINCE 1878, THANKS TO THE BERNISSART MINES IN BELGIUM, THE SITE OF A MAJOR DISCOVERY...

HOW ARE THE FRIES?

MAGNIFIQUE!

GRUMPH GHO

CHOMP

HMM...

ABOUT 30 PERFECTLY PRESERVED FOSSILS WERE RECOVERED THERE, TO EVERYONE'S DELIGHT...

WELL, ALMOST EVERYONE!

BRRRR!... YOUR STRANGE COAL DOESN'T HEAT!

WELL, YEAH, WE HAVEN'T UNEARTHED MORE THAN THIS FROM THE MINE AT THE MOMENT!

IGUANODON

MEANING: IGUANA TOOTH
PERIOD: EARLY CRETACEOUS (140-97 MILLION YEARS AGO)
ORDER/ FAMILY: ORNITHISCHIA/ IGUANODONTIDAE
SIZE: 30 FEET LONG
WEIGHT: 8,000-11,000 LBS.
DIET: HERBIVORE
FOUND: EUROPE, AMERICA

PLUMERI-BLOZ

DINOSAUR NAMES

IN 1824, AN ENGLISHMAN NAMED WILLIAM BUCKLAND WAS REALLY IRRITATED...

WHAT IS THIS FOSSIL, THEN?

YOU'RE WONDERING WHAT ITS NAME IS, MR. CUVIER*?

THUS, HE NAMED A DINOSAUR FOR THE FIRST TIME...

IT'S A HYPERMEGATOPS. NO, UM, A MEGATHING-- I'VE GOT IT! A MEGALOSAURUS!

THAT MEANS, "GIANT LIZARD!"

SINCE THAT DAY, HUNDREDS OF DINOSAURS HAVE BEEN GIVEN NAMES, PRIMARILY LATIN AND GREEK ONES...

...BASED ON A DISTINCTIVE PHYSICAL FEATURE...

STRUTHIOMIMUS, A DINOSAUR THAT'S "LIKE AN OSTRICH."

MORE ACCURATELY, AN OSTRICH LOOKS LIKE ME!

...THEIR SITE OF DISCOVERY...

ALBERTOSAURUS, DISCOVERED IN ALBERTA, CANADA.

HAVE A NICE DAY FROM ALBERTA.

...OR IN REFERENCE TO MYTHOLOGY.

DILONG, CHINESE "DRAGON EMPEROR."

MY NAME IS JUST TOO CLASSY!

IF THE SAME DINOSAUR HAS BEEN GIVEN DIFFERENT NAMES, WE RETAIN THE OLDEST ONE...

YUM! A HEDGE HOPPING HERBIVORE!

THAT'S WHY "BRONTOSAURUS" (THUNDER LIZARD) IS NOW CALLED APATOSAURUS (DECEPTIVE LIZARD).

OOPS! IT'S TOO BIG FOR ME!

AS FOR ME, I'VE GOT A SIMPLE METHOD OF NAMING DINOSAURS!

THIS ONE'S THE APPETIZER...

THIS ONE'S THE ENTRÉE...

AND THAT ONE'S DESSERT!

*GEORGES CUVIER, A FRENCH SCIENTIST WHO WAS INSTRUMENTAL IN ESTABLISHING THE FIELD OF PALEONTOLOGY.

EGG EATER (2)

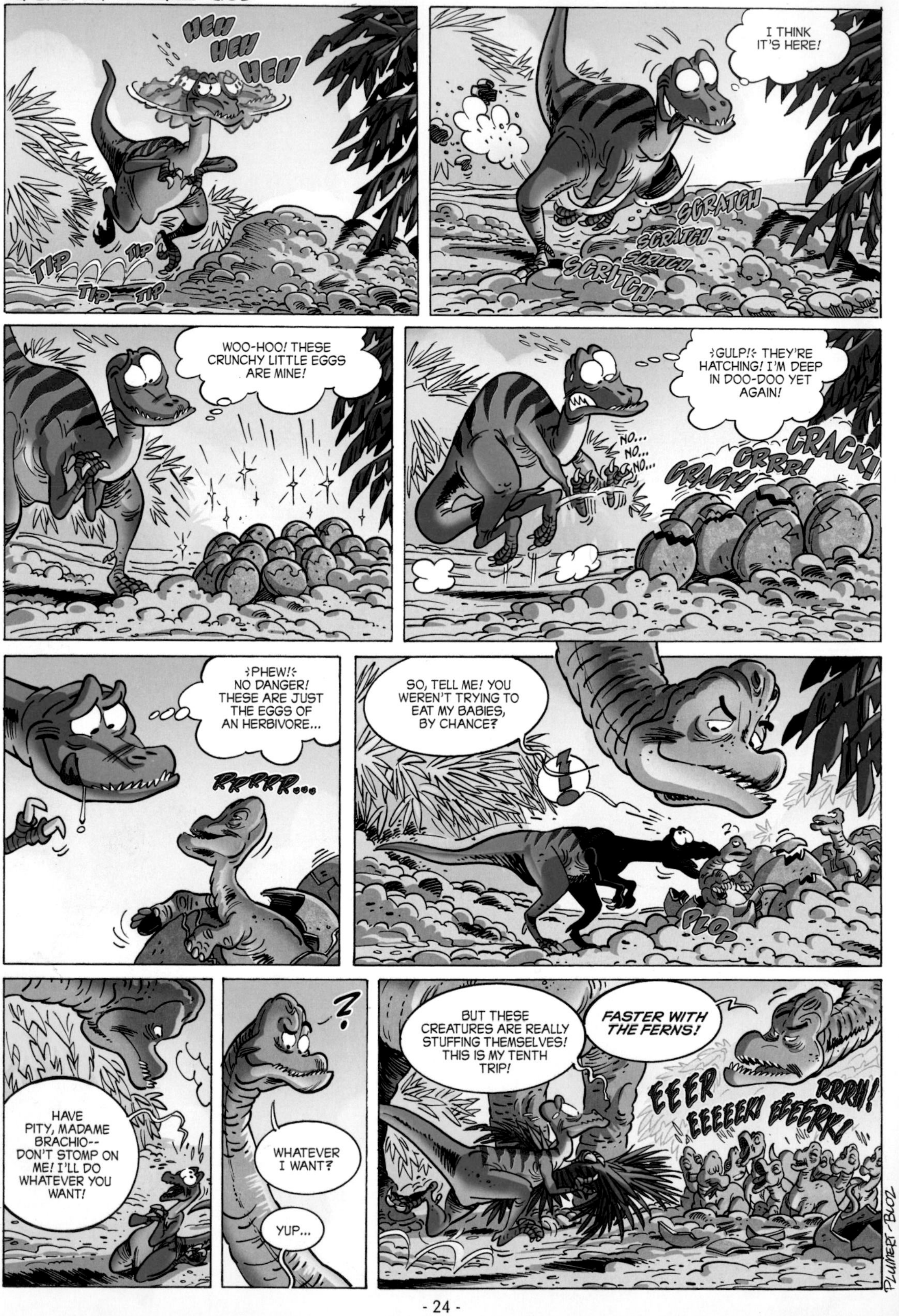

HEH
HEH
HEH
TIP
TIP
TIP
TIP
I THINK IT'S HERE!
SCRATCH
SCRATCH
SCRITCH
SCRITCH
WOO-HOO! THESE CRUNCHY LITTLE EGGS ARE MINE!
⁘GULP!⁘ THEY'RE HATCHING! I'M DEEP IN DOO-DOO YET AGAIN!
NO... NO... NO...
CRACK!
CRRR!
CRACK!
⁘PHEW!⁘ NO DANGER! THESE ARE JUST THE EGGS OF AN HERBIVORE...
RRRRR...
SO, TELL ME! YOU WEREN'T TRYING TO EAT MY BABIES, BY CHANCE?
PLOP
HAVE PITY, MADAME BRACHIO-- DON'T STOMP ON ME! I'LL DO WHATEVER YOU WANT!
?
WHATEVER I WANT?
YUP...
BUT THESE CREATURES ARE REALLY STUFFING THEMSELVES! THIS IS MY TENTH TRIP!
FASTER WITH THE FERNS!
EEER
RRRH!
EEEEEK!
EEEERK!

ALLOSAURUS

EN ROUTE TO A DINOSAUR AT LEAST AS AWESOME AS T. REX!

WOW!

IT'S CALLED *ALLOSAURUS!*

WHY WAS IT THE TERROR OF THE JURASSIC?

ALLOSAURUS

FIRST, BECAUSE IT EXISTED FOR MORE THAN 10 MILLION YEARS...

NORMALLY IT TAKES A WHILE TO EAT UP ALL THERE IS TO EAT...

TO EAT? SAY WHAT?

AND WE'VE FOUND TRACES OF THIS FINE GOURMET EVERYWHERE: THE U.S., EUROPE, AFRICA, AUSTRALIA...

NOT BAD, THIS AMERICAN "STEAK-OSAURUS!"

AND YES, ALLOSAURUS WAS THE REAL KING OF THE JURASSIC, BECAUSE NOTHING ON EARTH COULD STAND UP TO IT!

SLAP SLAP

?

GRRRR

MISTER, THIS DINO IS TOO MAJESTIC!

EVEN YOUR CAR CAN'T STAND UP TO IT!

MY JEEP!

ALLOSAURUS

MEANING: DIFFERENT LIZARD
PERIOD: LATE JURASSIC (156-144 MILLION YEARS AGO)
ORDER/ FAMILY: SAURISCHIA/ ALLOSAURIDAE
SIZE: 40 FEET LONG
WEIGHT: 4,000 LBS.
DIET: CARNIVORE
FOUND: U.S., EUROPE, AFRICA

PLUMERI - BLOZ

COPROLITES

THIS PALEONTOLOGIST IS ABOUT TO BRING A VALUABLE FOSSIL TO LIGHT...

A *COPROLITE*... IN OTHER WORDS, FOSSILIZED DINOSAUR DROPPINGS!

OH, SPLENDOR OF SPLENDORS!

THANKS TO THESE DROPPINGS, WE KNOW THE HERBIVORES AND THEIR FAVORITE PLANTS MUCH BETTER...

IT'S NOT *THAT* THAT'S GOING TO GET IT CONSTIPATED!

RECENTLY, A COPROLITE SOLD AT AUCTION FOR $1,000.00 AND YOU CAN FIND EVEN HIGHER PRICES!

WAHOO! I'M RICH!

WE FIGURED OUT THAT T. REX GROUND UP ITS PREY BEFORE DEVOURING IT FROM A 20 INCH-LONG, 15 LB. COPROLITE.

CHOMP CHOMP

CHEWING'S GOOD FOR THE DIGESTION!

CHOMP

INDEED, WE FOUND BITS OF BROKEN BONES IN ITS FECES.

MAGNIFICENT!

SO WHAT ARE YOU TELLING ME?

YOU REFUSE TO PICK UP THE PRESENTS YOUR DOG LEAVES?

PICK UP POOP? NO WAY!

THAT'S DISGUSTING!

AND BESIDES, I'M TOO BUSY EXAMINING *COPROLITES*!

PLUMERI & BLOZ

BIZARRE DINOSAURS

KIDS, I'M GOING TO SHOW YOU SOME REALLY STRANGE DINOSAURS...

OH OH WOW AH OH

LOOK AT THAT, FOR EXAMPLE. IT LOOKS LIKE A DRAGON'S HEAD. AND SO IT'S CALLED *DRACOREX*!

WOW!

BUT DOES IT SPIT FIRE? NOT REALLY...

:PRRT: :PRRT:

I'M A DRAGON!

!

ON THE OTHER HAND, ITS SKULL IS PERFECT FOR HEAD BUTTING!

BONK

I'LL TEACH YOU TO SPIT ON ME!

THE MALE *CRYOLOPHOSAURUS* HAD AN ODD CREST ON ITS HEAD...

WHAT A GOOD-LOOKING GUY!

...WHICH EARNED IT THE NICKNAME ELVISAURUS IN HONOR OF ROCK N' ROLL SINGER ELVIS PRESLEY.

LOVE ME, TENDER, LOVE ME TRUE...

IN TERMS OF CRESTS, THE *AMARGASAURUS* HOLDS THE RECORD FOR WEIRDNESS.

I'M SO CLASSY!

BUT HOW COULD IT STAY UPRIGHT WHEN THERE WAS TOO MUCH WIND?

I'M SO EMBARRASSED!

WHOOSH

BY EATING PLANTS, *STYRACOSAURUS* WAS UNDOUBTEDLY VERY TASTY...

I'LL SAY!

BUT ITS HEAD COULD CUT THE APPETITE OF ANY PREDATOR!

OOPS... I'D RATHER LOOK AT ITS BUTT!

KENTROSAURUS MUST OFTEN HAVE HAD PROBLEMS...

SAY IT ISN'T SO! YOU'VE BEEN HANGING OUT WITH THE PTERODACTYLS AGAIN!

?

...FAIRLY "PRICKLY" ONES.

HOW DID YOU KNOW?

TOO COOL!

AND YOU COULD SAY THAT ONLY A MOTHER COULD LOVE *NIGERSAURUS*...

YOU'RE HANDSOME WHEN YOU GRAZE, MY SON.

CRUNCH CRUNCH

...DUE TO ITS REALLY PECULIAR HEAD.

THANKS, MOM! *HEH, HEH, HEH...*

⸨ARGH!⸩ WHY'D I SAY THAT TO HIM?

AND FINALLY, A REAL TERROR...

CLUNK CLUNK CLUNK CLUNK

DILOPHOSAURUS

POGH SNIFF SNIFF

BA TA CRACK

...THE DOG!

DILOPHOSAURUS

YIII!!

RUMBER-BUOZ

- 28 -

ANKYLOSAURUS

ANKYLOSAURUS

MEANING: FUSED LIZARD
PERIOD: LATE CRETACEOUS (70-65 MILLION YEARS AGO)
ORDER/ FAMILY: ORNITHISCHIA/ ANKYLOSAURIDAE
SIZE: 33 FEET LONG
WEIGHT: 4,000 LBS.
DIET: HERBIVORE
FOUND: NORTH AMERICA

MATERNAL INSTINCT

WARNING! A WORRISOME CREATURE SEEMS TO BE TAKING AN INTEREST IN THESE BABY DINOSAURS...

FALSE ALARM! IT'S JUST A MAMA *MAIASAURA* FEEDING HER YOUNG.

ARE YOU CRAZY, SCARING MY KIDS?

WAA

WAA WAAH!

THIS TIME, DANGER! MAYBE THIS OVIRAPTOR FEELS LIKE HAVING A SMALL OMELET?

AH, NO! IT'S JUST A MOTHER INCUBATING HER EGGS.

TO THINK THAT MY NAME MEANS "EGG THIEF"!

I'M OUTRAGED!

FINALLY, A FEROCIOUS DINOSAUR, JUST THE WAY WE LIKE THEM! A HEARTLESS, KILLING MACHINE?

YYARR!

KWIK NAP

WRONG AGAIN! EVEN IF WE TEND TO THINK THEY WERE TOTALLY PITILESS...

MOM'S BACK!

YEAH! WITH OUR FAVORITE MEAT!

YUM! CORYTHOSAURUS!

IT'S IMPORTANT TO KNOW THAT MOST DINOSAURS LIKE THIS MAMA T. REX HAD A WELL-DEVELOPED MATERNAL INSTINCT!

HERE'S WHAT YOU ASKED FOR. I CAN'T DENY MY DARLING CHILDREN ANYTHING!

CRUNCH

YUM CRUNCH YARF WUM...

UNFORTUNATELY FOR THIS FEMALE, SOME FOLKS TRIED TO ABUSE HER MATERNAL STREAK!

BRING US ANOTHER BIG CREATURE!

FEED ME, MAMA!

THEY'RE BEGINNING TO WEAR ME OUT!

WE WANT TO EAT!

MOMMY, I'M HUNGRY!

AT HOME WITH THE PTEROSAURS

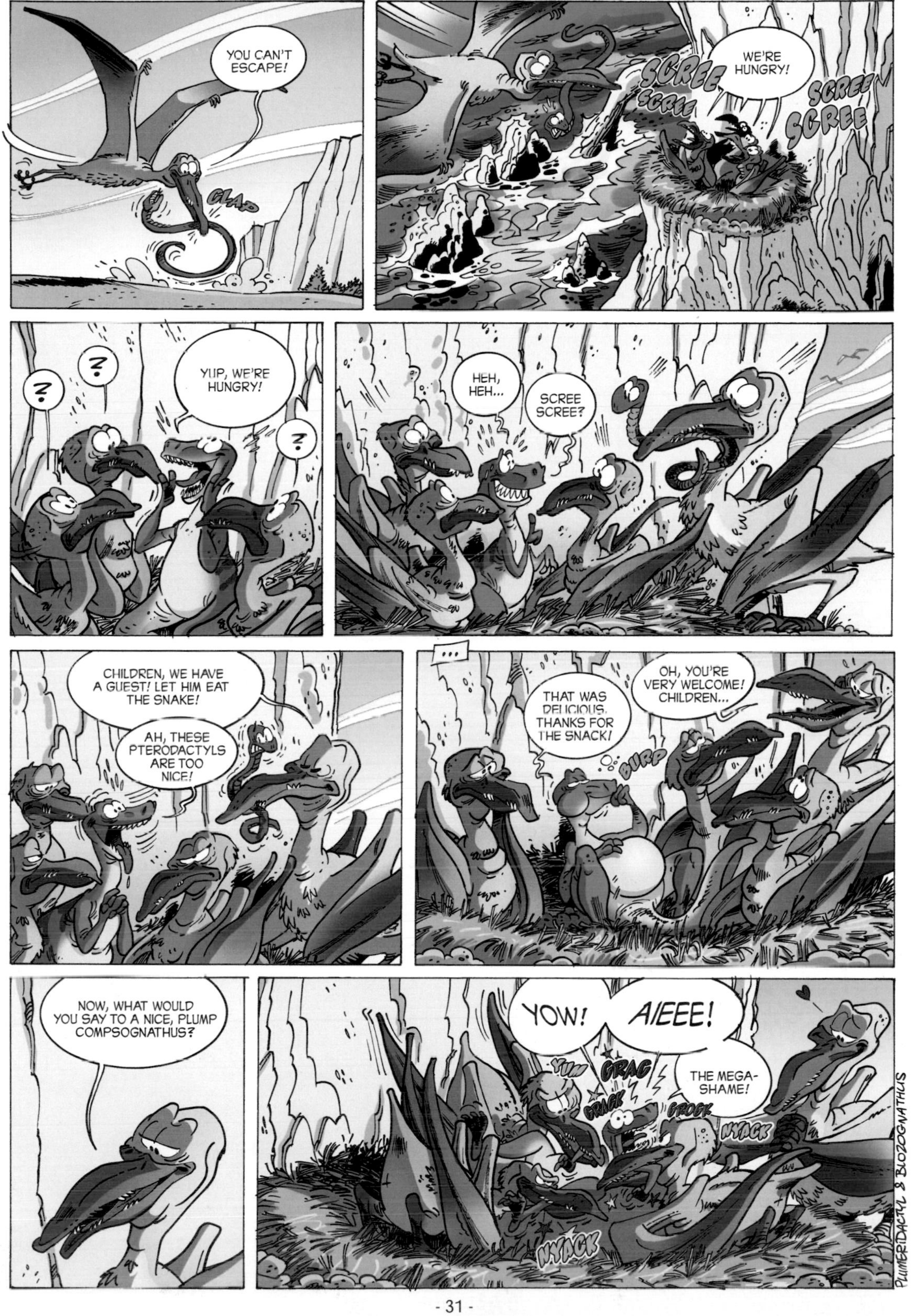

YOU CAN'T ESCAPE!
CLAP
SCREE SCREE
WE'RE HUNGRY!
SCREE SCREE
YUP, WE'RE HUNGRY!
HEH, HEH...
SCREE SCREE?
CHILDREN, WE HAVE A GUEST! LET HIM EAT THE SNAKE!
AH, THESE PTERODACTYLS ARE TOO NICE!
...
THAT WAS DELICIOUS. THANKS FOR THE SNACK!
BURP
OH, YOU'RE VERY WELCOME! CHILDREN...
NOW, WHAT WOULD YOU SAY TO A NICE, PLUMP COMPSOGNATHUS?
YOW!
AIEEE!
YUM
CRAC
CRACK
CROCK
THE MEGA-SHAME!
NYACK
NYACK
PLUMBRIDACTYL & BLOZOGNATHUS

MARINE REPTILES

WHEN DINOSAURS RULED THE EARTH, MARINE REPTILES DOMINATED THE OCEANS!

I'LL ATTEST TO THAT!

SOME MARINE REPTILES WERE ALMOST DINOSAURS, LIKE CROCODILES AND TURTLES, WHICH STILL EXIST TODAY...

WHAT? I'M GOING TO HAVE TO KEEP LIVING WITH THIS GLUTTON FOR *HOW* LONG?

ARCHELON, 13 FEET LONG.

DEINOSUCHUS, 40 FEET LONG.

HEH, HEH

BUT THE MAJORITY OF THEM DISAPPEARED, SUCH AS MOSASAURUS...

MOSASAURUS, 60 FEET LONG.

NO SURPRISE, HE'S GOING TO CHOKE ON MY SHELL.

ICHTHYOSAURUS, WHICH LOOKED LIKE A DOLPHIN...

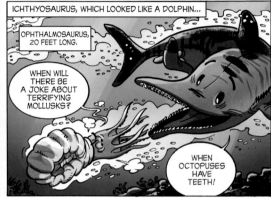

OPHTHALMOSAURUS, 20 FEET LONG.

WHEN WILL THERE BE A JOKE ABOUT TERRIFYING MOLLUSKS?

WHEN OCTOPUSES HAVE TEETH!

AND ALSO PLESIOSAURS, REPTILES WITH LONG NECKS.

THAT NECK WON'T GET ME OUT OF THIS JAM!

SNAP

ELASMOSAURUS, 46 FEET LONG.

INCIDENTALLY, ELASMOSAURUS IS PROBABLY THE ORIGIN OF THE LEGEND OF THE LOCH NESS MONSTER.

IT WOULD HAVE BEEN HIDING IN THIS SCOTTISH LAKE!

WELCOME TO THE LAND OF NESSIE

BUT DESPITE THE WARM LOCAL WELCOME, NESSIE NEVER SHOWS EVEN THE TIP OF ITS NOSE.

WEHWOOEH GOOEEW WEH

WEEEEE

WELCOME NESSIE

WELCOME TO THE NE

I WONDER WHY!

PLUMERI-BLOZ

PACHYCEPHALOSAURUS

THE SECRET TO A GOOD PACHYCEPHALOSAURUS?

IT ISN'T COMPLICATED-- YOU HAVE TO KNOW HOW TO USE YOUR HEAD.

I'LL SHOW YOU...

NOK NOK!

YOUR REINFORCED HEAD WILL HELP YOU GAIN THE RESPECT OF OTHER MALES...

SO WHO'S THE BOSS?

YOU'LL SEE-- LIFE WILL BE A LOT EASIER WITH FEMALES...

DID YOU UNDERSTAND THE FIRST LESSON, JUNIOR?

YES, YES! KNOW HOW TO USE YOUR HEAD!

UH, OH... SONNY, ANOTHER LESSON...

NO, NO! I GOT IT!

A MEGA HEAD-BUTT, JUST LIKE POPS!

GET OUT OF OUR TERRITORY, STINKY-MOUTH!

BONK

USING YOUR HEAD TO THINK ABOUT DANGER IS ALSO GOOD!

PACHYCEPHALOSAURUS

MEANING: THICK-HEADED LIZARD
PERIOD: LATE CRETACEOUS (70-65 MILLION YEARS AGO)
ORDER/ FAMILY: ORNITHISCHIA/ PACHYCEPHALOSAURIDAE
SIZE: 13 FEET LONG
WEIGHT: 1,000 LBS.
DIET: HERBIVORE
FOUND: NORTH AMERICA

PARASAUROLOPHUS

TERROR AMONG THE PARASAUROLOPHUS...

GROOAR

EEERK

A T. REX IS IN PURSUIT!

WHAT WILL BECOME OF THIS POOR FEMALE PARASAUROLOPHUS?

NOT PATÉ, I HOPE!

FOR HER, THESE HERBIVORES HAVE A FEW ASSETS-- THEY STICK TOGETHER...

?

AND THE MALES' ENORMOUS CRESTS, NEARLY 7 FEET LONG...

! **WOOOOOOOOOO WOO**

...LET THEM PRODUCE AMAZING SOUNDS!

LIKE A BLOODCURDLING FOGHORN, IT'S HARD TO WITHSTAND!

ENOUGH!

WOOOOOOOOOO WOOOOOO

MY HEROES!

IN OTHER CIRCUMSTANCES, SUCH A CHARACTERISTIC CAN, HOWEVER, HAVE SOME DRAWBACKS...

WOOOOO RZZZZZ... WOOOOOO RZZZZZ...OO WOO RZZZZZ

QUIET!

♪

THERE'S SOMEONE HERE WHO'D REALLY LIKE TO SLEEP!

PARASAUROLOPHUS

MEANING: LIKE CRESTED LIZARD
PERIOD: LATE CRETACEOUS (83-65 MILLION YEARS AGO)
ORDER/ FAMILY: ORNITHISCHIA/ HADROSAURIDAE
SIZE: 33 FEET LONG
WEIGHT: 4,000 LBS.
DIET: HERBIVORE
FOUND: NORTH AMERICA

PLUMERI & BLOZ

THE ANCESTORS OF BIRDS

SQUABBLING DURING THE JURASSIC...

RWEEEK

MAMA!

THERE'S A STRANGE DINOSAUR BUGGING ME!

CLUCK PUCK PUCK PICK

DID YOU SAY, "A DINOSAUR"? I ONLY SEE A BIRD!

THIS COMPSOGNATHUS HAS JUST DISCOVERED THE VERY ODD ARCHEOPTERYX...

COCKADO ODLEDOO!

HE'S WEIRD, ISN'T HE?

...WHICH HELPS PALEONTOLOGISTS DRAW THE LINE BETWEEN DINOSAURS AND BIRDS!

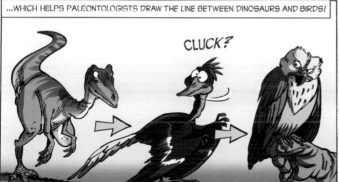

CLUCK?

AS A MATTER OF FACT, THEY SHARE MANY CHARACTERISTICS WITH COMPSOGNATHUS AND MODERN BIRDS.

WHAT? COUSIN?

I'VE GOT NOTHING TO DO WITH THIS FEATHERED EYESORE!

RIB RIB

ACHOO

BONKERS

UNBELIEVABLE! HE'S ALLERGIC TO FEATHERS, EVEN FOSSILIZED ONES!

STUDIO

NOW WE KNOW THAT THE STAR OF JURASSIC PARK, VELOCIRAPTOR, HAD FEATHERS!

SO, MR. SPIELBERG... YOU FORGOT TO GIVE US FEATHERS IN THE MOVIE?

PLUMEROZ

ORIGINALLY, FEATHERS WERE FOR KEEPING WARM.

‡BRR!‡-- WE'RE FREEZING-- ‡BRR!‡ OUR BUTTS, HERE! ‡BRR!‡

I'M NOT... HURRY UP AND DIE OF COLD! I'M HUNGRY!

THEN THEY BECAME MODIFIED SO THAT LIGHT DINOSAURS COULD FLY.

♪ I BELIEVE I CAN FLY!

LALALA TOUCH THE SKY...

HOP

OR PERHAPS, IN THE BEGINNING, TO GLIDE FROM TREE TO TREE.

SPLAT

WHEN BIRDS APPEARED, PTEROSAURS WERE NO LONGER MASTERS OF THE AIR.

WHAT ARE THESE COLORFUL THINGS?

SO IF YOU SEE THIS SCENE TODAY, IT'S COMPLETELY NORMAL...

HE'S NOT CRAZY! BIRDS ARE THE ONLY DINOSAURS THAT ARE STILL ALIVE!

AAAAH! A PIGEONOSAUR! IT'S GOING TO EAT US!

?

COOOO

OPEN

THAT'S ALL WELL AND GOOD, BUT THEY FORGOT TO SAY YOU CAN FLY, TOO, COMPSO!

ME? NO WAY!

YOU, WAY!

!

YOU SEE!

NOOOOOOOOOOOOOO

VAP

BLOUIN?

VELOCIRAPTOR

ONCE UPON A TIME, THERE WAS A SLIGHTLY STUPID *PROTOCERATOPS*...

THE DROMAEOSAURIDS! THE DROMAEOSAURIDS!

SAY WHAT? SAY WHO? WHY? YOU'RE LEAVING?

...WHO DIDN'T KNOW THAT THE MOST FAMOUS *DROMAEOSAURIDS* WERE...

RAPTORS!

HE DISCOVERED THEIR FAVORITE WEAPON RIGHT AWAY!...

HOLY COW! YOU DON'T CUT YOUR TOENAILS OFTEN ENOUGH!

VEU!!

AND THEIR FAVORITE WAY OF CHASING: STALKING...

PUFF...

GO AWAY!

PUFF... HELP!

PUFF...

...TO EXHAUSTION!

THAT'S GOOD! HE'S DONE FOR LET'S EAT!

ONCE UPON A TIME, THERE WERE SOME SLIGHTLY STUPID *VELOCIRAPTORS*...

?

?

?

..WHO DISCOVERED THAT *TARBOSAURUS* WAS A LAZY GUY.

NO FAIR! WE DID ALL THE WORK!

SSANKS, DUDES!

GIVE US BACK OUR MEAT!

VELOCIRAPTOR

MEANING: SWIFT THIEF
PERIOD: LATE CRETACEOUS (75-70 MILLION YEARS AGO)
ORDER/ FAMILY: SAURISCHIA/ DROMAEOSAURIDAE
SIZE: 7 FEET LONG
WEIGHT: 30 LBS.
DIET: CARNIVORE
FOUND: MONGOLIA, CHINA

PLURIRAPTOR & BIOCERATOPS

DIPLODOCUS

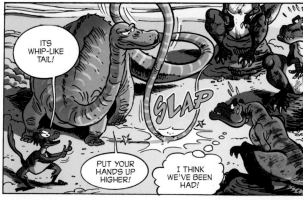

DIPLODOCUS

MEANING: DOUBLE BEAM
PERIOD: LATE JURASSIC (156-144 MILLION YEARS AGO)
ORDER/ FAMILY: SAURISCHIA/ DIPLODOCIDAE
SIZE: 100 FEET LONG
WEIGHT: 33,000 LBS.
DIET: HERBIVORE
FOUND: NORTH AMERICA

T. REX'S TEETH

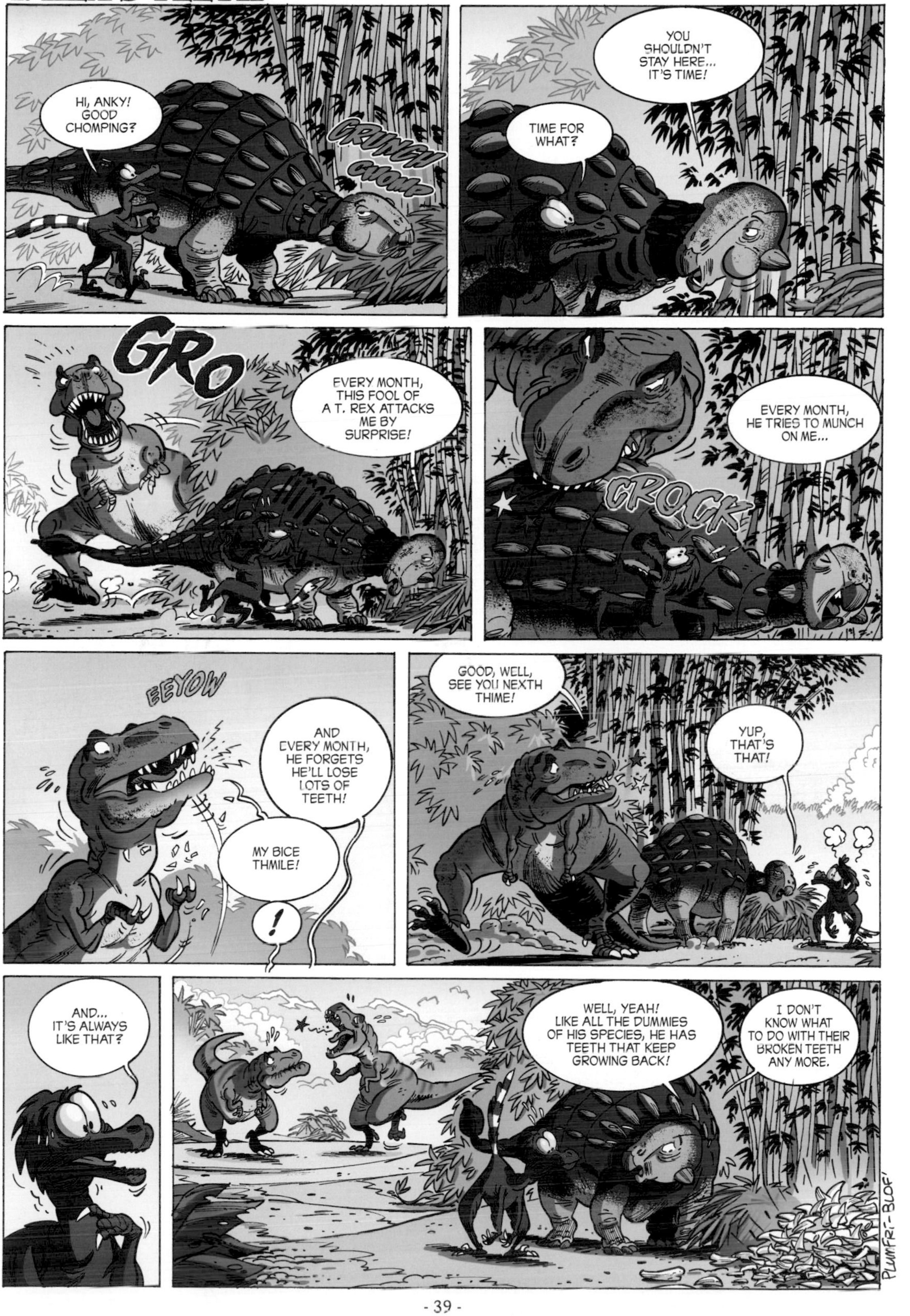
HI, ANKY! GOOD CHOMPING?
CRUNCH
CHOMP
YOU SHOULDN'T STAY HERE... IT'S TIME!
TIME FOR WHAT?
GRO
EVERY MONTH, THIS FOOL OF A T. REX ATTACKS ME BY SURPRISE!
EVERY MONTH, HE TRIES TO MUNCH ON ME...
CROCK
EEYOW
AND EVERY MONTH, HE FORGETS HE'LL LOSE LOTS OF TEETH!
MY BICE THMILE!
!
GOOD, WELL, SEE YOU NEXTH THIME!
YUP, THAT'S THAT!
AND... IT'S ALWAYS LIKE THAT?
WELL, YEAH! LIKE ALL THE DUMMIES OF HIS SPECIES, HE HAS TEETH THAT KEEP GROWING BACK!
I DON'T KNOW WHAT TO DO WITH THEIR BROKEN TEETH ANY MORE.
PLUMFRI-BLOF!

DINOSAUR TRACKS

AMAZING! IN OUR TIME, WE STILL FIND DINOSAUR TRACKS!

SET DOWN IN SOFT SOIL, THESE TRACKS GIVE US LOTS OF INFORMATION.

CAREFUL NOT TO SLIP! MUDDY TERRAIN COMING UP!

PARTICULARLY ABOUT THE SIZE OF THEIR MAKERS.

DON'T MUDDLE ME WITH YOUR MATH!

HEIGHT AT THE SHOULDERS = 4 X THE LENGTH OF THE FOOTPRINT

20 FEET

THE ORGANIZATION OF THEIR HERD...

ELDERLY AND DISABLED TO THE REAR! YOUTHS IN THE CENTER! CUTE FEMALES NEXT TO ME!

NO FAIR!

AND ALSO THE SPEED OF THEIR TREK... AND OF THEIR PURSUERS.

MAMA!

AFTERWARDS WE'LL TALK ABOUT THE TRACKS OF MY TEETH, OKAY?

ALLOSAURUS: 25 MILES/ HOUR MAX.

YOUNG BRACHIOSAURUS: 5 MILES/ HOUR MAX.

SUPER! MUD! ME, TOO! I WANT TO LEAVE A MARK ON HISTORY!

COMPSO

ONE SMALL STEP FOR A COMPSOGNATHUS, AND A GIANT LEAP FOR...

!

SPLOTCH

AND HERE'S THE MOST RIDICULOUS PRINT LEFT BY A DINOSAUR!

THE MEGA-SHAME!

OURANOSAURUS

FINDING A GREAT PLACE TO EAT IS NEVER EASY, EVEN IF YOU'RE AN OURANOSAURUS...

HELLO THERE, MATE! WHAT ARE YOU DOING?

SLURP

I'M DYING OF THIRST, SO I'M LICKING THE PLANTS...

HOW ABOUT YOU-- INTERESTED IN A LITTLE SIP OF MOSS?

SLURP

NO NEED TO LICK THE MOSS WHEN THERE'S A RIVER RIGHT HERE!

WE'RE NO FOOLS!

OH, NO! DON'T GO THERE, WHATEVER YOU DO!

POOR FOOLS!

WHAT? SINCE THE DEATH OF SPINOSAURUS, WE'RE NOT AFRAID OF ANY OTHER DINOSAURS...

IT'S TRUE-- THERE ARE NO MORE KILLER DINOSAURS LEFT AROUND HERE...

?

BUT THERE'S SARCO, THE GIANT CROCODILE!

EEEK!

I WOULDN'T BE AGAINST A LITTLE SIP OF MOSS, MYSELF!

SARCOSUCHUS IMPERATOR, 40 FEET LONG

OURANOSAURUS

MEANING: BRAVE LIZARD
PERIOD: EARLY CRETACEOUS (115-110 MILLION YEARS AGO)
ORDER/ FAMILY: SAURISCHIA/ IGUANODONTIDAE
SIZE: 23 FEET LONG
WEIGHT: 8,000 LBS.
DIET: HERBIVORE
FOUND: WEST AFRICA

PLUMERI & BloZ

THE DISAPPEARANCE OF THE DINOSAURS

INDINO JONES ANSWERS YOUR QUESTIONS

AND WHY DID YOU STEAL SANTA'S BEARD?

HEY, MISTER! WHY DID THE DINOSAURS DIE?

AH, WELL, WE DON'T REALLY KNOW WHY THE DINOSAURS DISAPPEARED... BUT HERE ARE A FEW SLIGHTLY WACKY HYPOTHESES...

AND DO YOU KNOW WHAT MY BEARD SAYS TO YOU?

HYPOTHESIS 1: THE INTENSE ACTIVITY OF SUPER-VOLCANOES...

HUZZAH!

SPEWED FLOODS OF LAVA AND SULFUR, POLLUTING THE ATMOSPHERE, WATERING HOLES, AND VEGETATION, KILLING THE DINOSAURS.

RUNNING AWAY ALREADY? YOU FINALLY FIGURED OUT WHO'S THE BOSS?

HYPOTHESIS 2: THE APPEARANCE OF FLOWERING PLANTS, A BIG NOVELTY FOR THE DINOSAURS.

WHAT'S THIS THING? CAN IT BE EATEN?

SNIFF

THE PLANTS WOULD HAVE POISONED THE HERBIVORES.

THEY SAY TO EAT FIVE FLOWERS AND VEGGIES EVERY DAY!

AND WITHOUT HERBIVORES TO SNACK ON...

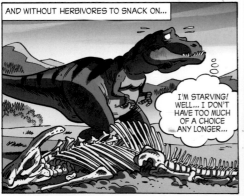

OOO

I'M STARVING! WELL... I DON'T HAVE TOO MUCH OF A CHOICE ANY LONGER...

...THE CARNIVORES WOULD HAVE DIED NEXT.

:CHOKE!: THESE PLANTS ARE SO DISGUSTING THEY WILL KILL YOU!

GRUMBL ARGH

YUCK GUGHZ

HYPOTHESIS 3: (TOTALLY LUDICROUS): MEDDLING BY EXTRATERRESTRIALS WHO WERE JEALOUS OF THE DINOSAURS' ACHIEVEMENTS!

MEH! IT'S HIDEOUS! ZAP IT, KODOS!

?

HYPOTHESIS 4: RETREATING OCEANS. AS NEW LAND APPEARED, THE SEASONS BECAME TOO HOT OR TOO COLD.

FASTER, TROODONS!

DO YOU WANT TO KILL US, REX?!

HYPOTHESIS 5: CLIMATE CHANGE CAUSED BY VOLCANOES AND FOREST FIRES.

HEY! IT SEEMS LIKE IT'S CLOUDING OVER!

ACID RAIN WOULD HAVE DESTROYED THE EARTH.

:ARGGH!: THAT BURNS! MY EYES!

MY WONDERFUL EYES!

PSHEE

PSHEE

HYPOTHESIS 6: THE EMERGENCE OF MAMMALS, WHO WOULD HAVE DEVOURED THE DINOSAURS' EGGS.

GRUNCH KRUNCH

HEY, YOU!

I'LL TEACH YOU TO EAT MY EGGS!

HYPOTHESIS 7: OR MAYBE THEY WERE VICTIMS OF AN EPIDEMIC?

ACHOO

ACHOOOO PLOP

SORRY-- I'VE GOT A COLD!

BUT THE MOST PLAUSIBLE HYPOTHESIS: THE IMPACT OF A GIANT METEORITE 65.5 MILLION YEARS AGO.

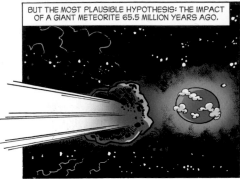

WE'VE FOUND ITS TRACES IN MEXICO: THE CHICXULUB CRATER IS 6 MILES IN DIAMETER!

CHICXULUB?!

BLESS YOU!

I DIDN'T SNEEZE: THAT'S THE NAME OF THE TOWN!

ACHOOO

SUCH AN IMPACT WOULD HAVE HAD THE SAME EFFECT AS SEVERAL ATOMIC BOMBS!

CAUSING A SERIES OF CATASTROPHES: GIGANTIC TSUNAMIS, VOLCANIC ERUPTIONS, AND ACID RAIN DESTROYING PLANTS AND ANIMALS.

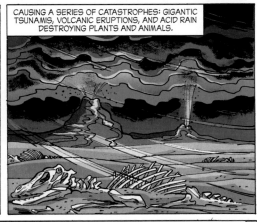

AND THE ASHES CAUSED BY THE IMPACT WOULD HAVE MASKED THE SUN'S RAYS FOR YEARS...

...MARKING THE END OF THE DINOSAURS, AFTER A REIGN OF OVER 160 MILLION YEARS!

HELP ME!
ME-- ME-- ME-- METEORITES!

OH, GEEZ, CAN'T SOMEONE POOP IN PEACE ANY LONGER AROUND HERE?

YUCK!
THAT'S DISGUSTING! I WOULD'VE PREFERRED METEORITES!

PLUMERI, PICE & BLOZIOSAURUS.

T. REX, INVINCIBLE DINOSAUR?

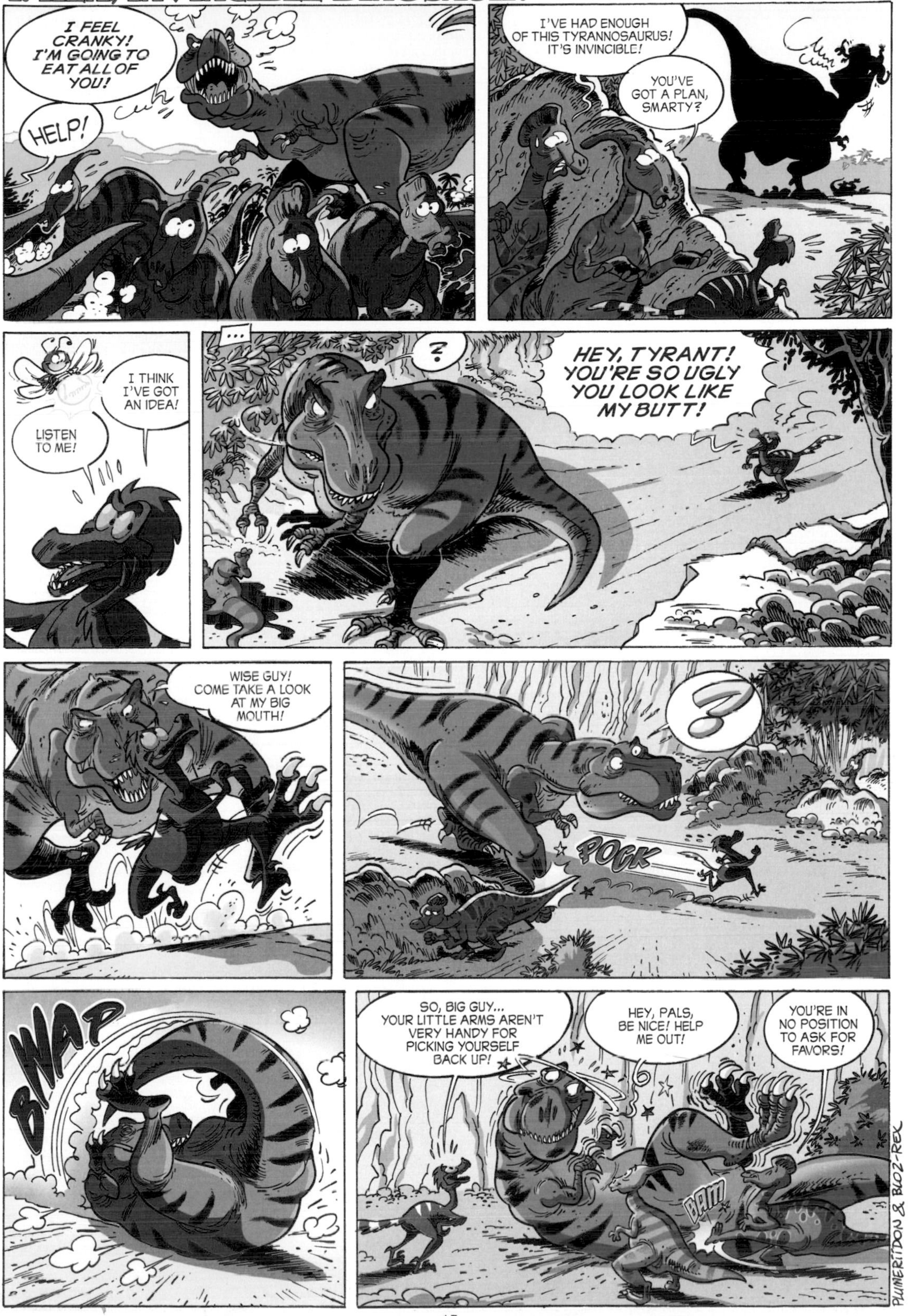
I FEEL CRANKY! I'M GOING TO EAT ALL OF YOU!
HELP!
I'VE HAD ENOUGH OF THIS TYRANNOSAURUS! IT'S INVINCIBLE!
YOU'VE GOT A PLAN, SMARTY?
I THINK I'VE GOT AN IDEA!
LISTEN TO ME!
...
?
HEY, TYRANT! YOU'RE SO UGLY YOU LOOK LIKE MY BUTT!
WISE GUY! COME TAKE A LOOK AT MY BIG MOUTH!
?
POCK
BWAP
SO, BIG GUY... YOUR LITTLE ARMS AREN'T VERY HANDY FOR PICKING YOURSELF BACK UP!
HEY, PALS, BE NICE! HELP ME OUT!
YOU'RE IN NO POSITION TO ASK FOR FAVORS!
BAM
PLUMERI'DON & BLOZ-REX

MAMMALS

ONE OF OUR DISTANT ANCESTORS WENT OUT INTO THE LAND OF THE DINOSAURS...

GO ON OUT, CHILDREN! THE COAST IS CLEAR!

IN THIS ERA, TO SURVIVE THE DINOSAURS, IT WAS BEST TO BE DISCREET...

SUU!

...VERY FAST...

RAAAAR

EEEEK!

DADDY!

WAAH

...AND TO HAVE MANY CHILDREN, IN ORDER TO PERPETUATE THE SPECIES!

YOU ROTTEN SCUM! I'LL AVENGE MY FATHER!

RHHH RHHH SQUEAK

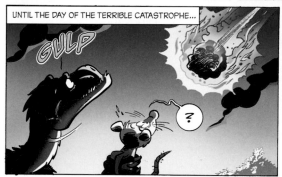

UNTIL THE DAY OF THE TERRIBLE CATASTROPHE...

GULP

?

...THAT EXTERMINATED THE DINOSAURS AND ALMOST ALL LIFE ON THE PLANET...

WOOOOOSH

BUT NOT OUR DISTANT COUSINS!

THE REIGN OF THE MAMMALS ON EARTH COULD FINALLY BEGIN!

REVENGE! I'M THE KING OF THE WORLD!

SHH! NOT SO LOUD!

WATCH OUT FOR PAPERCUTZ™

Welcome to the fossilized, first DINOSAURS graphic novel from Papercutz, those upright-walking mammals dedicated to publishing great graphic novels for all ages! I'm Jim Salicrup, your Editor-in-Chief and last surviving dinosaur. Everyone at Papercutz hopes you enjoyed this graphic novel, and if you're looking for more dinosaur-filled comics fun, may I suggest, that in addition to the next volume of DINOSAURS (#2 "Bite of the Allosaurus") that you also check out…

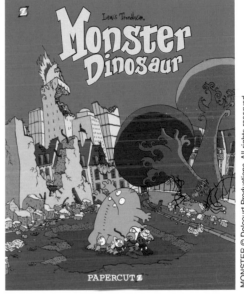

MONSTER #3 "Monster Dinosaur" by Lewis Trondheim. It's the story of an almost ordinary family… and their pet monster. In this particular volume, Dad and the kids create dinosaurs to battle each other to the death! Oh, and it's a very funny series.

GERONIMO STILTON #7 "Dinosaurs in Action" Geronimo's a time-traveling mouse, who saves the future, by protecting the past. And this time, he travels all the way back to the Cretaceous period to battle those pesky Pirate Cats! All sorts of dinosaur fun ensues! Check out the special excerpt starting on the next page!

For more exciting news on what's happening at Papercutz, be sure to visit our website, and we'd love to hear from you too! Just check out the box below on how to contact us.

Until next time, watch out for DINOSAURS #2 "Bite of the Allosaurus." (That's just got to hurt!)

Thanks,

JIM

STAY IN TOUCH!

EMAIL: salicrup@papercutz.com
WEB: www.papercutz.com
TWITTER: @papercutzgn
FACEBOOK: PAPERCUTZGRAPHICNOVELS
MAIL: Papercutz, 160 Broadway,
      Suite 700, East Wing, New York, NY 10038

Special Excerpt from GERONIMO STILTON #7 "Dinosaurs in Action"!

WHILE IN THE CRETACEOUS PERIOD...

ZOOOOMM

SPLASH

STOP HOLDING YOUR BREATH, YOU MOUSE-BRAIN!

YOU KNOW THE CATJET'S AMPHIBIOUS!

YOU DO, BUT I DON'T!

ALL THIS WATER GIVES ME THE WILLIES!

MEOW DOWN*, BONZO. WE'VE LANDED!

*CALM DOWN.

I HOPE YOU LIKE IT HERE, PROFESSOR, BECAUSE YOU'RE GOING TO BE STAYING A VERY LONG, LONG TIME!

WELCOME TO THE CRETACEOUS PERIOD!

HELP! LET GO OF ME!

AS YOU WISH, PROFESSOR!

OUCH!

THUMP

NO! I DON'T WANT TO STAY HERE! PULL ME BACK UP!

GLADLY, RIGHT AWAY!

HEE, HEE! IT'S LIKE A YO YO!

CRASH

STOP PLAYING AROUND!

?!?

COME ON, DITCH THE MOUSE AND LET'S LEAVE!

DID YOU SEE WHAT I SAW?

YES!

A FISH!

?!?

NOW'S MY CHANCE TO SLIP AWAY...

THE BIGGEST I'VE EVER SEEN!

...BEFORE THOSE NASTY CATS FEED ME TO THE FISH!

WE NEED A FISHING POLE!

FIRE UP THE COALS!

WHAT'RE YOU THINKING OF, YOU FATHEADS?

WHICH MEANS: A HUGE FEAST!

THAT FISH IS HUGE!

BUT... THAT'S A PREHISTORIC ANIMAL!

SO IT IS! AND WE'LL BE THE FIRST CATS IN THE WORLD TO HAVE THE MOST MEMORABLE PIG-OUT IN HISTORY!

MORE THAN THAT... IN PREHISTORY!

PLOTOSAURUS

THE NAME OF THIS AQUATIC REPTILE THAT LIVED IN THE CRETACEOUS MEANS "FLOATING LIZARD." WITH A LENGTH OF UP TO AROUND 42 FEET, IT HAD A TAPERED BODY, THE END OF ITS TAIL WAS IN THE SHAPE OF A RHOMBUS, AND IT HAD LARGE EYES THAT GAVE IT EXCELLENT UNDERWATER VISION.

B-BUT... WE NEED TO LEAVE AND FINISH OUR MISSION!

YUM! MY MOUTH IS WATERING!

CRACK

THIS LONG STICK WILL DO THE JOB FOR US!

DO WHAT YOU WANT... BUT, JUST SO YOU KNOW, PROFESSOR VON VOLT HAS ALREADY RUN OFF!

WHA-!?

YEAH, HE'S GOING TO BE STUCK HERE, JUST AS WE PLANNED!

INSTEAD LET'S THINK...

BAH! WHO CARES ABOUT THAT MOUSE NOW?

SWISS

I SEE IT! I SEE IT! CAST THE BAIT!

...ABOUT GETTING OURSELVES AN AFTERNOON SNACK!

~GROAN!~ I SMELL THE STINK OF TROUBLE!

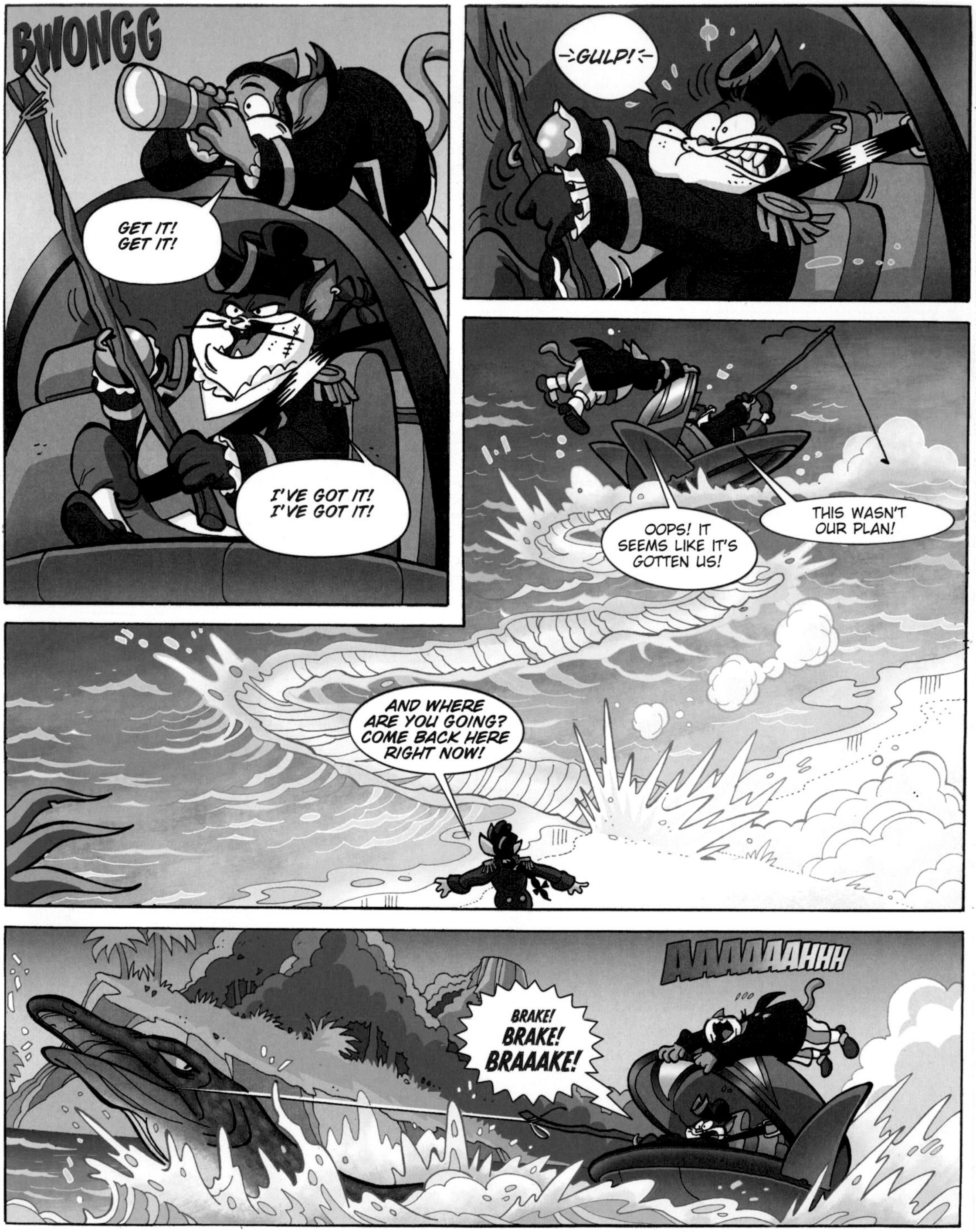
BWONGG
GET IT! GET IT!
I'VE GOT IT! I'VE GOT IT!
GULP!
OOPS! IT SEEMS LIKE IT'S GOTTEN US!
THIS WASN'T OUR PLAN!
AND WHERE ARE YOU GOING? COME BACK HERE RIGHT NOW!
AAAAAAHHH
BRAKE! BRAKE! BRAAAKE!

Don't Miss GERONIMO STILTON #7 "Dinosaurs in Action"!

Index of Terms

Carnivore: an animal that eats meat.

Coprolite: fossilized animal droppings.

Cretaceous: era between 145 and 65 million years ago.

Dinosaur: term created by Sir Richard Owen that means "fearfully great lizard." Dinosaurs were reptiles but had their own distinctive characteristics. (For example, they held their legs directly under their bodies.) All dinosaurs were land-based: none flew and none lived in the water.

Fossil: an animal or vegetable solidified in rock.

Herbivore: an animal that lives on plants. The term, "vegetarian," is probably more appropriate than "herbivore," as herbs and grass only appeared a little while after dinosaurs became extinct.

Jurassic: era between 200 and 145 million years ago.

Mammal: an animal with mammary glands, whose females nurse their young.

Ornithischian: a dinosaur with hips like a bird.

Paleontology: the science that studies extinct species. Its specialists are paleontologists.

Piscivore: an animal that eats fish.

Plesiosaur: a marine reptile that was almost a dinosaur.

Predator: an animal that attacks its prey to eat it.

Pterosaur: a flying reptile that was almost a dinosaur.

Reptiles: vertebrates that primarily crawl. They currently include crocodiles, lizards, snakes, turtles, and used to include dinosaurs, pterosaurs, and plesiosaurs.

Saurischian: a dinosaur with hips like a lizard.

Triassic: era in which dinosaurs appeared, between 250 and 200 million years ago.

Continued on next page…

G L O S A R Y

Allosaurus (Page 25)
Meaning: Different lizard
Period: Late Jurassic (156-144 million years ago)
Order/ Family: Saurischia/ Allosauridae
Size: 40 feet long
Weight: 4,000 lbs.
Diet: Carnivore
Found: U.S., Europe, Africa

Ankylosaurus (Page 29)
Meaning: Fused lizard
Period: Late Cretaceous (70-65 million years ago)
Order/ Family: Ornithischia/ Ankylosauridae
Size: 33 feet long
Weight: 4,000 lbs.
Diet: Herbivore
Found: North America

Brachiosaurus (Page 16)
Meaning: Arm lizard
Period: Late Jurassic (160-145 million years ago)
Order/ Family: Saurischia/ Brachiosauridae
Size: 80 feet long
Weight: 110,000 lbs.
Diet: Herbivore
Found: Africa, America, Europe

Compsognathus (Page 11)
Meaning: Elegant jaw
Period: Late Jurassic (156-140 million years ago)
Order/ Family: Saurischia/ Compsognathidae
Size: 3 feet long
Weight: 6 ½ lbs.
Diet: Carnivore
Found: Germany, France

Deinonychus (Page 15)
Meaning: Terrible claw
Period: Early Cretaceous (120-98 million years ago)
Order/ Family: Saurischia/ Dromaeosauridae
Size: 10 feet long
Weight: 175 lbs.
Diet: Carnivore
Found: North America

Diplodocus (Page 38)
Meaning: Double beam
Period: Late Jurassic (156-144 million years ago)
Order/ Family: Saurischia/ Diplodocidae
Size: 100 feet long
Weight: 33,000 lbs.
Diet: Herbivore
Fossils: North America

Iguanodon (Page 22)
Meaning: Iguana tooth
Period: Early Cretaceous (140-97 million years ago)
Order/ Family: Ornithischia/ Iguanodontidae
Size: 30 feet long
Weight: 8,000-11,000 lbs.
Diet: Herbivore
Found: Europe, America

Ouranosaurus (Page 41)
Meaning: Brave lizard
Period: Early Cretaceous (115-110 million years ago)
Order/ Family: Saurischia/ Iguanodontidae
Size: 23 feet long
Weight: 8,000 lbs.
Diet: Herbivore
Found: West Africa

Pachycephalosaurus (Page 33)
Meaning: Thick-headed lizard
Period: Late Cretaceous (70-65 million years ago)
Order/ Family: Ornithischia/ Pachycephalosauridae
Size: 13 feet long
Weight: 1,000 lbs.
Diet: Herbivore
Found: North America

Parasaurolophus (Page 34)
Meaning: Like crested lizard
Period: Late Cretaceous (83-65 million years ago)
Order/ Family: Ornithischia/ Hadrosauridae
Size: 33 feet long
Weight: 4,000 lbs.
Diet: Herbivore
Found: North America

Spinosaurus (Page 19)
Meaning: Spiny Reptile
Period: Late Cretaceous (108-94 million years ago)
Order/ Family: Saurischia/ Spinosauridae
Size: 50 feet long
Weight: 15,000 lbs.
Diet: Carnivore and piscivore
Found: Northern Africa

Stegosaurus (Page 13)
Meaning: Roof lizard
Period: Late Jurassic (156-140 million years ago)
Order/ Family: Orinthischian/ Stegosauridae
Size: 30 feet long
Weight: 11,000 Lbs.
Diet: Herbivore
Found: North America

Therizinosaurus (Page 21)
Meaning: Scythe lizard
Period: Late Cretaceous (70-65 million years ago)
Order/ Family: Saurischia/ Therizinosauridae
Size: 30 feet long
Weight: 13,000 lbs.
Diet: Herbivore
Found: China, Mongolia

Triceratops (Page 9)
Meaning: Three-horned face
Period: Late Cretaceous (68-65 million years ago)
Order/ Family: Ornithischia/ Ceratopsidae
Size: 30 feet long
Weight: 20,000 lbs.
Diet: Herbivore
Found: North America

Troodon (Page 8)
Meaning: Wounding tooth
Period: Late Cretaceous (75-65 million years ago)
Order/ Family: Saurischia/ Troodontidae
Size: 6.5 feet long
Weight: 110 lbs.
Diet: Carnivore
Found: North America

Tyrannosaurus rex (Page 5)
Meaning: Tyrant lizard king
Period: Late Cretaceous (68-65 million years ago)
Order/ Family: Saurischia/ Tyrannosauridae
Size: 35-50 feet long
Weight: 11,000 lbs.
Diet: Carnivore
Found: North America

Velociraptor (Page 37)
Meaning: Swift thief
Period: Late Cretaceous (75-70 million years ago)
Order/ Family: Saurischia/ Dromaeosauridae
Size: 7 feet long
Weight: 30 lbs.
Diet: Carnivore
Found: Mongolia, China

Diplodocus　　**Ankylosaurus**　　**Parasaurolophus**